DATE DUE

MAR 1 3 1994			
JAN 2 6 1997			
JUN 1 6 2002			
SEP 2 2 2002			
Dec 28			
FEB - 5 2006			
MAR 2 7 2011			

PRINTED IN CANADA

GRANDMA
I'll Miss You

A Child's Story about Death and New Life

Words by
Kathryn Slattery

Pictures by
Renée Graef

Chariot Books™
David C. Cook Publishing Co.

Lo! I tell you a mystery. We shall not all sleep,
but we shall all be changed, in a moment,
in the twinkling of an eye....
I CORINTHIANS 15:51, 52

Chariot Books™ is an imprint of David C. Cook Publishing Co.
David C. Cook Publishing Co., Elgin, Illinois 60120
David C. Cook Publishing Co., Weston, Ontario
Nova Distribution Ltd., Newton Abbot, England

GRANDMA, I'LL MISS YOU: A CHILD'S STORY ABOUT DEATH AND NEW LIFE
©1993 by Kathryn Slattery for text and Renée Graef for illustrations

Scripture is quoted from the Revised Standard Version of the Bible, ©1946, 1952,
1971, 1973.

Designed by Gary Gnidovic

First Printing, 1993
Printed in Malaysia
97 96 95 94 93 5 4 3 2 1

Library of Congress Cataloging-in-Publication Data
Slattery, Kathryn.
Grandma, I'll Miss You ... a child's story about death and new life / by Kathryn Slattery.
     p. cm.
Summary: Eight-year-old Katy is saddened by the fact that her grandmother is dying,
but Grandma explains that her soul will be moving on to a wonderful new life in heaven.

ISBN 0-7814-0937-3
(1. Death—Fiction. 2. Christian life—Fiction. 3. Grandmothers—Fiction.) I. Title
PZ7.S629Gr 1993
(E)—dc20   92-18984
                                                                CIP
                                                                AC

For Katy and Brinck,
and children of all ages, everywhere…

Happy and sad.

That's how Katy felt.

Very happy and very sad. In fact, in all her eight years, Katy had never felt so mixed-up. Katy was happy because her mother was going to have a baby. "Soon," her mom said, patting her big tummy. "The doctor tells me the baby will be born very soon."

But Katy was sad because her grandmother—her most favorite person in the world—was dying.

"Can you believe it?" Grandma said, shaking her white-haired head in disbelief. "The doctor tells me I've precious little time left on this good earth. Well, old girl," she patted Katy's hand, "if that's true, we'd better make the most of it!"

Katy's grandma had always called Katy "old girl." Katy didn't know why, but she knew she liked it.

Now, she wondered how her grandma could be so matter-of-fact—almost cheerful—about such bad news.

But then, Katy reminded herself, *Grandma always had been different.*

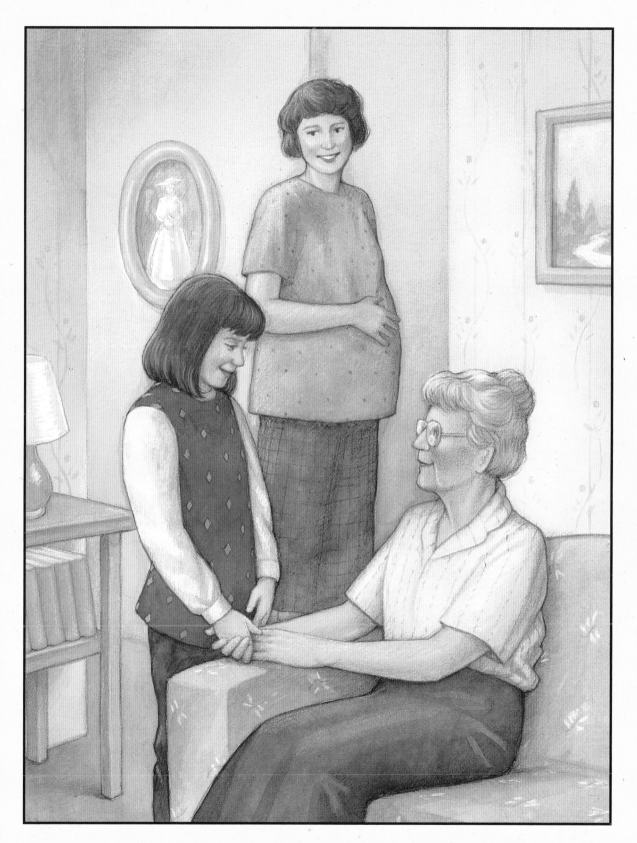

To begin with, there was the mysterious matter of her age. For as long as Katy could remember, Grandma had claimed to be "thirty-nine and holding." According to the records kept in the old family Bible, Katy figured Grandma was actually eighty-two years old. "Age," Grandma liked to say, "is all in the mind. You're as old as you think you are. Remember that, old girl."

Grandma's eyes were clear blue and sparkly, like two bright marbles, and when she smiled (which was practically all the time) a thousand tiny lines crinkled around them like rays of sunshine.

Grandma's hands were old and gnarled and veiny, like the branches of an old apple tree. But her touch, as she brushed away Katy's bangs when they needed cutting (which was practically all the time) was soft as the petals of a rose.

She didn't wear much jewelry. Just the wedding ring Grandpa had given her more than half a century ago, and a tiny silver cross that had belonged to her younger sister, Mabel, who died of appendicitis when she was only twelve years old. "That was back in the old days before there were wonder drugs like today," Grandma said.

Whenever she talked about Grandpa (who had died before Katy was born) or her sister, Mabel, Grandma always got a faraway look in her eyes. "How I wish you could have known them, old girl," she would say to Katy. "My, how you would make them laugh!"

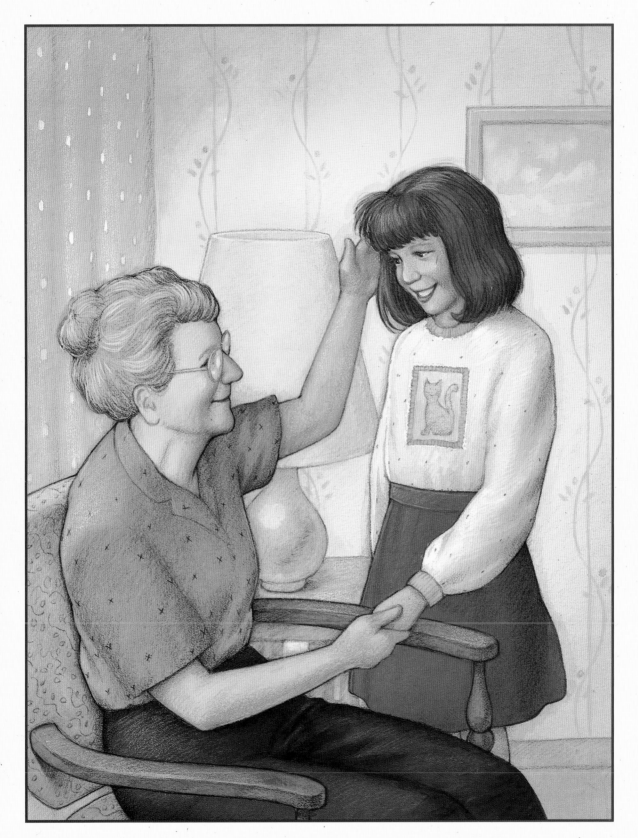

seven

And Grandma smelled so good. Like cinnamon and nutmeg and vanilla. One day Katy caught her in the kitchen, actually using vanilla, straight from its little brown bottle, as perfume. "When I was a girl about your age," Grandma grinned, "I was desperate to wear perfume and rouge like my older sisters, but Ma forbid me. So I pinched my cheeks till they were pink, and dabbed vanilla behind my ears. Here," she passed the bottle to Katy, "try a little for yourself."

Grandma knew how to do things no one else did. Like make old-fashioned pearl tapioca pudding from scratch. "'Fish eyes in glue,'" Grandma said, standing at the kitchen stove, stirring the sweet gooey mixture as it bubbled merrily in the glass double boiler. "That's what my brothers used to call my mother's tapioca. Can you imagine? Oh, those boys used to tease poor Ma something terrible." Grandma laughed and shook her long-handled wooden spoon at Katy. "Now don't you dare go repeating that to your younger brother!"

And everyone looked forward to Saturday mornings when Grandma made her famous deep-fried buttermilk doughnut holes. It was Katy's job to shake the crisp, warm, fragrant balls in a big brown paper bag filled with powdered sugar. "No one shakes that bag like you, old girl," Grandma would say.

Somehow Grandma always seemed to know the right thing to say.

One Christmas, Katy's favorite gift was a pet hamster. But no one—not even her dad, who usually liked animals—wanted to have anything to do with the furry little creature. "Get that rodent away from me," her dad said gruffly, backing away in alarm when Katy held the hamster up to his face for closer inspection. "*Ee-e-k!*" squealed Katy's mom. "It looks too much like a mouse for me!" As for her little brother—well, all he wanted to do was feed the hamster to his pet snake.

But not Grandma.

"Cute little critter," she said, extending a crooked finger to stroke the hamster's velvet-soft, quivering nose. "Is it a girl or a boy? Have you decided on a name? Why, if you ask me, it looks just like a miniature teddy bear."

Back in the old days, Grandma used to live in town in a big old three-story Victorian house on Main Street. The house had a wide, wraparound front porch with white wicker chairs and a love seat with faded, flowery cushions. The fancy wooden trim that decorated the outside of the house was called "gingerbread," and in the summertime Grandma always had lots of hanging baskets with red and pink geraniums. "Peppermint plants," Grandma liked to call them, "to go with my gingerbread house."

But a few years after Grandpa died, Grandma sold the big house and moved in with Katy's family. Ever since Katy could remember, Grandma's bedroom had been upstairs, down the hall and catty-corner from Katy's room. Sometimes, when both their doors were cracked open just right, Katy and Grandma would wave good night to each other from their beds.

But now Grandma was dying.

And not even the arrival of a new baby could take away the deep sadness Katy felt.

What will happen to Grandma when she dies? Katy wondered. *Is there really such a place as heaven? Will we ever get to see each other again?*

t h i r t e e n

One night, Katy was sitting on the family room sofa between her mom and Grandma. The television set was turned off, and the three were taking turns feeling the baby's kicks and punches within Katy's mom's big tummy.

"Oo-o-o-o! Did you feel that?" her mom grinned. "That was an uppercut, I think. Or maybe a left jab. This little person is a real fighter!"

Grandma smiled. But it was a tired smile. And—it seemed to Katy—a sad smile.

"Grandma," Katy said, "are you afraid about dying?"

"Katy!" scolded her mom. "Don't ask such questions."

"Now, now," said Grandma. "Let the girl ask what she likes. It's good to talk."

She cupped her gnarled hands around Katy's.

"Yes, old girl, sometimes I am afraid. I know so much more about life on earth than I do about the new life waiting for me in heaven. But it's perfectly normal to be afraid about things we don't fully understand. It helps when I try to remember that death, in its way, is as natural a part of life as birth. In fact, there's a lot we can learn about death from birth."

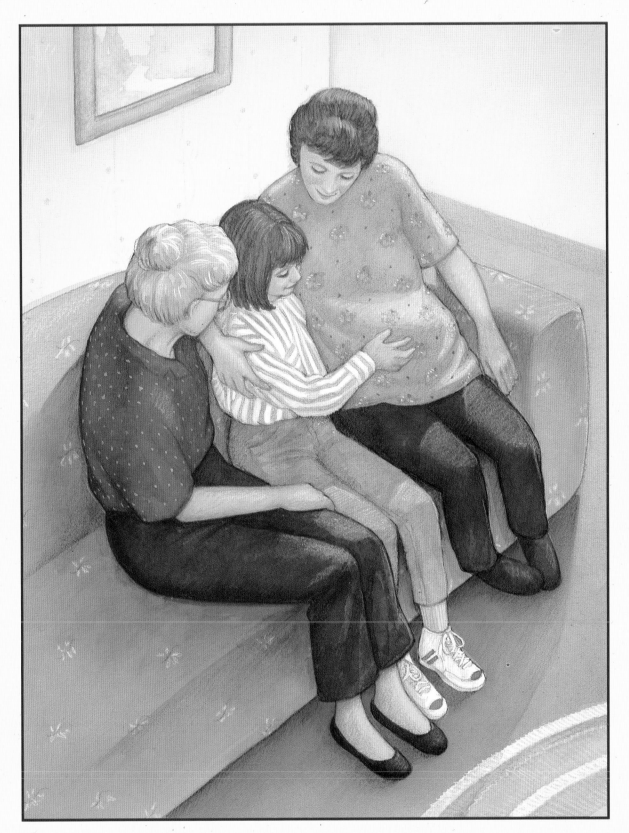

fifteen

Grandma took Katy's hands and placed them on her mom's tummy.

"Think for a moment about this baby here, all cozy and warm, safe and snug in the darkness of your mother's womb," she said.

"Pretend for a moment that this baby can talk. And pretend that you've just told this baby that—whether he liked it or not—a mysterious experience called birth was about to happen to him, and that when it did happen, he would be entering a world unlike anything he could ever imagine.

"Well, I think this baby would probably say something like, 'What? Leave my safe, warm world that I love and know so well, and have spent my whole life in, for some bright, noisy place I know nothing about? No way!'

"Angry and scared. That's how the baby would most likely feel. Crazy as it may seem, the unborn baby might even have the mistaken idea that what was about to happen to him wasn't birth at all, but *death*—in the sense that everything about life as he knew it was going to come to an abrupt end.

Because how can you begin to explain to an unborn baby the glorious colors of flowers in spring . . . or the magic of dancing rainbows cast by sunlit crystal . . . or fireworks on the Fourth of July? How can you explain to an unborn baby the beauty of Mozart being played on the piano . . . the sound of laughter . . . the taste of a chocolate ice-cream cone with sprinkles . . . the smell of fresh-baked cinnamon bread . . . the downy softness of a hamster's nose? How can you explain to an unborn baby the way powdered sugar melts to sweetness on the tip of your tongue? The excitement of Christmas Eve? The way it feels to wake up on your birthday morning? The way it feels to be caught in the middle of a family hug, happily squished between your mother and father, like the filling of a sandwich?

n i n e t e e n

No," Grandma shook her head, "I don't think that what is going to happen to me is death. I like to think of it as *birth*—birth to a new life in a new and wonderful world called heaven. A world more beautiful and full of love and good feelings than anything I've ever known. A world that here and now—like an unborn baby—I can barely begin to imagine."

"But how do you know you're going to heaven, Grandma?" Katy asked.

"Ever since I was a little girl, I've believed in God and Jesus, and in the promises in the Bible," said Grandma. "Ma and Pa taught me that faith was a good and helpful thing to have, and that the Bible was like a guidebook for living. In the Bible it says, *'For God loved the world so much that he gave his only son, Jesus, so that whoever believes in him will not die, but will live with him forever.'* That's a promise—and not just for me, but for you, too. And for your mom and dad and brother, and for Grandpa who died already, and for the little baby here who hasn't been born yet. It's God's promise for everyone in the world."

Where is heaven, Grandma? What's it like? Who's there? Will I ever see you again?"

"So many questions, old girl. So many questions. . . ." Thoughtfully, Grandma fingered the tiny silver cross that hung around her neck.

"Heaven," said Grandma, "isn't here on earth. Except maybe, in our hearts. The way it feels when we love someone, and when we know deep down inside that we are loved back. Then I think we get a glimpse. Take you and me, for instance. Now, there's a bit of heaven, don't you think?"

Katy nodded. Her heart felt like it was going to burst she loved her grandma so much.

"As human beings here on planet earth," Grandma went on, "God places each of us in time and space for a special purpose. We are born, we live our lives the best we can, and then, when our adventure on earth is over, we die. But heaven is outside time and space. It's like another dimension. We know from the Bible that God our Father has been there always. And Jesus. And all the angels. It is a wonderful place full of love and peace and forgiveness and joy. *'In heaven,'* the Bible says, *'God will wipe away every tear from every eye.'*

"Personally," said Grandma, "I like to think of heaven as a big birthday party."

Her blue eyes sparkled.

And I almost forgot the best part. When I get to heaven, I'll get a brand-new body."

Katy and her mom were speechless at this bit of news.

"Now don't you two girls look so surprised," grinned Grandma. "This old body you see here isn't the real me, you know. It's just a container, a shell, for my soul, which is the invisible, real me that will go to heaven and live forever. And it's the same for you. Here on earth, our human bodies aren't designed to last forever. Over time they tend to wear out and get old and sick, like mine. Or they meet with a sudden illness or an accident. When this happens and our bodies die, there's a wonderful, mysterious moment when our souls are released to heaven. And once our souls are in heaven, they're wrapped in new bodies—very special bodies that will never get sick, never get old, never feel pain, and will last forever."

"But how?" asked Katy. "How does all that happen? What does it feel like?"

Grandma wrapped her arm around Katy and pulled her close.

"Now that," she said, her blue eyes twinkling, "is a *mystery*. A mystery so special that we each have to wait and discover the true meaning of it ourselves, each in our own way, when we die."

The room grew quiet.

No one moved or said a word.

Even the baby was still.

Oh, Grandma," Katy said, "I'm going to miss you so much when you die."

"And I'll miss you, too, old girl. If there's any way God can keep me up to date on what's happening in your life here on earth, I'm sure He will. It helps knowing that we'll all be together again one day in heaven. Remember, that's a *promise*."

She closed her eyes.

"I'm very tired now, dear," she said. "It's best I get myself upstairs and try to get some sleep."

That night, the bedroom doors were cracked open just right so Katy could glimpse Grandma in her bed. The light on her bedstand was on, and she was sitting upright, propped against two plump pillows. Her long white hair hung down around her small shoulders so that from a distance she almost looked like a young girl. Her glasses were low on her nose, and in her hands was a plain black book. She was reading her Bible.

Suddenly, as though sensing Katy's glance, she looked up, and smiled. Then she lifted her hand and waved. Katy waved back.

Good night, Grandma, she thought. *I sure do love you.*

And for a moment she was almost certain she heard Grandma say, "And I love you, too, old girl."

A warm breeze ruffled the curtains and the sun was streaming through Katy's windows as she awoke. Opening her eyes, she was startled to see her mom sitting at the foot of her bed.

"Grandma . . ." her mom's voice was barely a whisper.

Katy's heart felt sick, and she was filled with a sense of dread at what she knew her mom was about to say.

"Grandma died last night." It was hard for her mom to even say the words. "The doctor says her old heart finally just stopped beating. The doctor says she didn't feel any pain—"

Katy watched as her mother's face crumpled with grief, and felt her own throat tighten and her eyes fill with tears. The sense of loss and sadness she felt was so deep and hurt so badly.

"Oh, Mom," Katy cried, wrapping her arms around her mother, "we're going to miss Grandma so much!"

She hugged her mom tightly, and the two of them rocked back and forth, back and forth on the bed, murmuring words of comfort to each other and letting their tears flow.

At the same time, Katy kept thinking of Grandma and her new life in heaven. . . .

What must it be like, with God and Jesus and all those angels? And Grandpa, and her sister, Mabel, and her ma and pa, and all her other sisters and brothers and friends who had died before. . . . What a grand reunion they must all be having! Like a big birthday party. . . .

What was it Grandma had said?

Death, in its way, was as natural a part of life as birth.

Though Katy knew she would miss her grandma terribly, she was comforted somehow by this thought.

Yes, it was true Grandma had died. But her soul was forever alive!

Like the baby that would soon be born into this world, Grandma was beginning a new and wonderful love-filled life . . . in heaven.